Brownies

For Anna, with thanks for all
her help and hard work

STRIPES PUBLISHING
An imprint of Magi Publications
1 The Coda Centre, 189 Munster Road,
London SW6 6AW

A paperback original. First published in Great Britain in 2010
Published by arrangement with Girlguiding UK
Brownie logo, uniforms and badges copyright © Girlguiding UK
Text copyright © Caroline Plaisted, 2010. Illustrations copyright © Katie Wood, 2010

ISBN: 978-1-84715-140-7

A CIP catalogue record for this book is available
from the British Library.

Printed and bound in the UK.
2 4 6 8 10 9 7 5 3 1

Find out more about the author at
www.carolineplaisted.com

Brownies

Christmas Cheer

Stripes

Meet the Brownies

Katie

Katie, Grace's twin, is super sporty and likes to play games and win. She wants to get every Brownie badge and her Six is Foxes!

Jamila

Jamila's got too many brothers, so she loves Brownies because NO BOYS ARE ALLOWED! Jamila is a Badger!

Ellie

Awesome at art and crafts, Ellie used to be a Rainbow and likes making new friends. Ellie is a Hedgehog!

Animal-crazy Charlie has a guinea pig called Nibbles. She loves Brownie quizzes and Pow Wows. Her Six is Squirrels!

Charlie

Grace

Grace is Katie's twin sister and she's ballet bonkers. Grace enjoys going on Brownie outings, and she is a Rabbit!

Chapter 1

"Brrr! Isn't it cold," exclaimed Ellie, as she arrived at the school hall for Brownies. She pulled open the door, and her four best friends followed her inside.

"Freezing," agreed Charlie. "Luckily, Gran finished my new mittens just in time for winter!"

"They're so cool," said Jamila, admiring Charlie's red and white snowflake mittens as the girls took off their coats.

Just then, the hall door opened again.

"Hey, look – Daisy's back," said Katie, rushing over to say hello to the Young Leader, who had her video camera bag slung

over her shoulder. Daisy had been away for a
week on a Guide trip.

"I wonder why Daisy's brought her video
camera," said Grace.

But before she could go over and ask,
Vicky, one of the Brownie Leaders, called
out, "Over to your Six tables to do some
activity sheets, Brownies! Pow Wow in
ten minutes."

The 1st Badenbridge Brownies were made
up of five Sixes, and Katie, her twin sister
Grace, and their best friends Ellie, Jamila and
Charlie were all in different ones. A few
months before, their unit had held an open
evening so other girls could come and find
out what fun Brownies was. Five new
members had joined as a result. Tayla-Ann

had joined the Rabbits, Grace's Six. She loved gymnastics and had impressed all her new Brownie friends when she showed them some of the medals and certificates she had won in competitions.

The newest member of the Squirrels, Charlie's Six, was Ruby. Ellie knew her from an art club she had been to in the school holidays, so was really pleased when Ruby had joined their Brownie unit.

The Foxes, which was Katie's Six, had welcomed Leah to their group. She had two younger sisters who had already put their names down to join the Brownies when they were old enough.

Ellie's Six, the Hedgehogs, had Abebi as their new member. She'd moved to the area a few months before and had joined Badenbridge Primary. Lastly, Danuta was in the Badgers with Jamila. She'd arrived from Poland earlier that year, and the girls had been especially excited when they discovered that she'd been a Brownie in Poland too! Like Abebi, Danuta had joined Badenbridge Primary, and she was on the same netball team as Katie.

All the Brownies, old and new, were now busy at their Six tables, working on some activity sheets. They were about choosing which clothes to wear, and the Brownies had to match up pictures of clothes with the right season to wear them.

Meanwhile, over at the stage side of the hall, Daisy, Vicky and Sam, the other Brownie Leader, were setting up the hall's projector screen. It looked like the Brownies were going to watch a film!

"Tidy away, girls," Sam called out. "Let's get into the Brownie Ring!"

Moments later, the girls were sitting in a circle, eager to find out what was happening next.

"As you know, Daisy's back from her trip to Foxlease," said Vicky. "Foxlease is a special Training and Activity centre in Hampshire, for those Brownies who don't know."

"So what did you do there?" Grace asked.

"You remember I've been taking photos and filming all the things we got up to for the Centenary?" Daisy replied. "Well, I was doing that as part of my Adventure 100 badge,

to preserve guiding for the future."

All the 1st Badenbridge Brownies had chosen to take part in Adventure 100 and had completed a series of adventures to celebrate Girlguiding UK's Centenary. Even their Leaders had joined in. Now, the Brownies wore their Adventure 100 badges on their sashes and gilets with pride.

"That's so cool," sighed Katie. "But what were you doing with the films and photos?"

"We were learning how to edit them together to make a complete history of the year," said Daisy.

"It's a really good film," said Sam, "and we thought you'd like to see it!"

"Yes, please!" said the Brownies.

"Come on then," said Vicky. "Turn round to face the screen. I'll switch off the lights, and then Daisy – it's over to you!"

The film captivated the Brownies. They saw themselves making things and learning new games, taking part in badge activities, climbing the clock tower at the town hall, flying kites, and dancing and singing as they zoomed around town for their Dance Dash. There was also footage of a few of the older Brownies with Daisy's Guide unit at the Centenary BIG GIG – a huge concert that had started off the Centenary year. The last bit of the film showed the girls renewing their Promise alongside all the other Brownies, Rainbows and Guides in their District at Vision, the final event of the Centenary year and the launch of the next 100 years.

"Hey, look – that's us!" Charlie pointed out, as she caught sight of their unit in the huge crowd of girls who had gathered at Badenbridge Manor.

As the film finished, the Brownies and their Leaders clapped and cheered.

"That was brilliant!" said Boo, Charlie's older sister.

"Even we were in the film," said Abebi, turning to Tayla-Ann and the other new girls.

"Thank you, Daisy. That was great," said Vicky, smiling. She switched the lights back on and looked at her watch. "Right! We should crack on."

Quickly, the girls got back into the Brownie Ring.

"So, has anyone got any news?" asked Sam.

Immediately, Grace and Caitlin put up their hands.

"We've got shared news," said Grace.

"We went to some dance auditions a little while ago, and yesterday we heard that we've both been chosen to appear in a pantomime

this Christmas!" announced Caitlin.

The other Brownies grinned excitedly.

"That's brilliant," said Vicky. "Tell us more!"

"It's *Cinderella*," said Caitlin, "and it'll be on at the theatre in Robertstown."

"That's the same show we're seeing for the District outing," Katie pointed out. "So we'll get to see Caitlin and Grace on stage!"

"Wow!" said the Brownies, impressed.

"Do you know who else is going to be in it?" asked Lucy.

"Trina Bliss from *Century Village*, that soap on telly," said Grace. "And Chester Chuckles – you know, the really funny man who is in the panto every year?"

"And Jez Simons, who presents *Kid Zone*, is going to be Buttons!" said Caitlin.

"Cool," said Boo.

"So what are you two going to be doing?" asked Bethany.

"We'll be dancing and singing in the chorus," said Grace.

"Well done, girls," said Vicky. "I think you both deserve a special clap."

All the Brownies cheered, and Grace and Caitlin grinned happily.

"Talking of the panto," Sam continued, "if you want to come, you'll need to get a parent or guardian to sign the permission slips we gave you last week. We need the slips back next week so we can book the tickets!"

"All this talk about the pantomime reminds me of something else we've got to look forward to," Vicky added.

The Brownies glanced at each other excitedly. What could that be?

Chapter 2

"It's just over four weeks until Christmas…" Vicky continued.

The Brownies smiled at the thought. Everyone loved Christmas!

"Which means the Brownie Christmas party is coming!" Sam finished. "It'll be a chance for all of us to wear our party clothes and eat loads of yummy food."

"Yes," Vicky said. "We'll talk a bit more about that nearer the time. But can one of the older Brownies remember what else we do at this time of year?"

Izzy put up her hand. "We make Christmas present boxes," she said.

Sam nodded. "Every year, we put together some Christmas present boxes to send to children who are living in difficult circumstances in countries around the world. Children who haven't got proper homes to live in because of conflict or natural disasters, like earthquakes."

"You mean like in Haiti?" asked Ellie.

"Exactly," replied Vicky. "So who can tell us more about the boxes?"

Boo put up her hand. "We use an empty shoebox, covered in Christmas wrapping paper," she explained. "We put in things like soap, toothpaste and a toothbrush."

"Plus some kind of toy," said Faith.

"We've got a leaflet about it for you to take home tonight, so you can decide if you'd like to take part," said Sam.

The best friends looked at each other and smiled. It was their first Christmas as Brownies and they thought the boxes sounded like a great idea.

"We've also got a new event this year," added Vicky, looking round the hall at all the eager faces. "There's going to be a Christmas market in the town hall."

"There'll be stalls selling all sorts of Christmassy things, such as cards, seasonal food, soaps and gifts. And, of course, Father Christmas will be there too!" explained Sam. "We've been asked to go along and sing Christmas songs to add to the festive feeling!"

The Brownies cheered.

Sam giggled. "So you'd like to do it then?"

The Brownies replied with an even louder cheer.

"Terrific!" said Vicky. "The organisers have arranged for us to have a collection box so when people hear how beautifully we sing, they'll hopefully give a donation to the Badenbridge charity for the homeless.

There'll be a letter for your parents to take home when they collect you. But now it's time for our first Christmas craft session."

The Brownies sat up, excited.

"We're each going to make a Christmas card," Sam explained. "We've got glitter pens, stick-on gems – lots of sparkly things."

"This is a special card that we'd like you to give to someone who has been an important part of your Centenary year. So, as you are making it, think about who that might be," added Vicky.

"Let's get busy!" said Sam, and the Brownies rushed off to their Six tables.

The girls had great fun designing their cards. They drew Christmas trees, snowflakes, robins – all sorts!

When they had finished, they put them carefully into their Brownie bags to keep them safe. Then, after an exhausting game of Traffic Lights, it was time to go home.

"Only four weeks until Christmas!" sighed Grace, as she buttoned up her coat.

"I can't wait," said Ellie, tucking the letter about the Christmas market into her bag.

"Nor me," agreed Charlie. "And I can't wait for tea at Jamila's tomorrow either!"

Jamila was working towards her Cook badge, and had asked her best friends round for tea to help eat the feast of cookies she'd baked.

Katie opened the hall door to find their parents were waiting for them. "Brr! I'm putting my gloves on. It's chilly out there!"

Chapter 3

Jamila's mum met the girls after school the next day, and they walked back to the house together. The best friends arrived to find a large plate, piled high with cookies, on the kitchen table.

"Did you make all of these?" said Grace.

Jamila nodded. "Tuck in!"

"Yum!" said Katie, munching on a cookie.

"They're as great to look at as they are to eat," said Ellie, licking icing off her fingers.

Jamila had used writing icing to decorate the cookies with the girls' names, as well as colourful Brownie Trefoils.

25

"Have you nearly finished your Cook badge now?" asked Charlie.

Jamila nodded. "Almost. I still need to finish my scrapbook, and I'm going to make some more cookies to take to Brownies next week as part of my badge work."

"Oooh," said Ellie, licking her lips. "You should make cookies for the Christmas party!"

"Yes!" said Grace. "Ones that look like Father Christmas."

"Or Christmas trees!" added Charlie.

"That would be cool," agreed Jamila.

"So what's in your scrapbook?" asked Grace, who'd also made one when she did her Dancer badge.

"Have a look," said Jamila, taking it from the shelf and handing it to Grace. "Mum has taken photos of me cooking, to show that I know how to be safe in the kitchen."

"You look like you're doing the washing up here," said Charlie, showing it to the others.

Jamila giggled. "I was! I had to clear the table too. Plus I've talked to Vicky about food hygiene."

"Wow!" said Katie, finishing off the last cookie. "You've had to work really hard. But you're nearly there now."

"There's one other thing," said Jamila. "I've also got to make lunch or breakfast for three or four people."

"Hey, how about we have a sleepover and you could make breakfast," suggested Ellie.

"Yes, please!" exclaimed the others.

"Good idea," said Jamila. "I'll speak to Mum and see if we can arrange it for one weekend soon."

"So how are the preparations going for the panto, Grace?" Charlie asked.

"We haven't started rehearsals yet," Grace explained. "But Caitlin and I have met the other girls and boys who are in the chorus. And we'll be meeting the stars soon too!"

"It's just brilliant that it's the same panto we're going to see," said Ellie. "I can't wait!"

"Nor me!" giggled Grace, standing up and doing a twirl.

The weather grew chillier over the next couple of days, and everyone in Badenbridge wrapped up warm when they went outside. The best friends started to feel as though Christmas really was on its way, especially because festive preparations had started at school, too. Rehearsals for the Christmas concert began, and their teacher asked them to come up with some ideas for how they would like to decorate their classroom.

On Friday afternoon, sleet began to fall, and the five friends were pleased to be in Ellie's cosy living room where they were talking about the charity Christmas present boxes.

"I've bought a few things to put in my shoebox," Ellie said. "Some toiletries, pencils and paper, and lots of hair ties and pretty clips."

"That sounds lovely," Grace said. "Katie and I thought we'd put some tights and socks in our boxes."

"Good idea," said Charlie. "Hey, do you think the boxes will be sent to places as cold as here?"

"Some of them will be," Katie replied. "But even places that are warm in the day can get really chilly at night."

"Like when the sun went down when we were on Brownie camp," added Charlie. "I was thinking I might put a woolly scarf in my box."

Ellie gasped. "That's what we should do! We should make our own scarves to put in. My mum's got some wool we could use."

"But I can't knit!" said Charlie.

"Nor can we," added the twins.

"Do you think your mum could teach us?" asked Jamila, who liked the idea of making something special to add to the present box.

"I'm sure she could – let's go and ask!" said Ellie.

The girls raced into the kitchen and told Ellie's mum their idea.

"I'd be happy to teach you to knit, girls," Ellie's mum smiled. "It'd be fun! But it will take you a while to knit a whole scarf. Do you think you can finish it in time for the Christmas present box deadline?"

"Well, we could ask our own mums for help," Katie pointed out.

"Yes!" The others nodded.

"Come on then," said Ellie's mum. "Let's get out the knitting needles and choose what colour wool you'd like to use."

The five friends spent a happy, cosy afternoon learning how to knit. It took a while for them to get the hang of finishing a stitch without dropping it off the end of the needle, though.

When their mums came to collect them that evening, the girls told them all about their new project. And the grown-ups were just as excited as their daughters!

"We'll have to tell Gran," Charlie's mum said. "She'll be thrilled to hear you're learning to knit!"

"I've got some spare wool at home," added Jamila's mum. "I haven't knitted for ages – it would be nice to do something creative during these chilly evenings!"

Katie and Grace's mum agreed. "Tell you what," she said. "Why don't you all come round to ours tomorrow afternoon and we could all sit and knit together!"

So on Saturday afternoon, while wintry rain fell outside, the five friends and their mums gathered at Katie and Grace's house. They sipped warming hot chocolate and worked

on their scarves. The mums helped when the girls got stuck, and busied themselves with their own knitting projects too.

"That was fun," Charlie said, when it was time to go home.

Ellie nodded. "Brownies always gives us good ideas about things to do, even when we aren't at a meeting," she said.

And her four friends agreed. Being a Brownie made things extra good fun!

On Monday morning, before the start of the school day, Katie, Grace, Jamila and Ellie were playing a skipping game in the playground to help them keep warm, when Charlie came racing up.

"I had another idea for Brownies last night!" she announced. "I was thinking about the

Christmas present boxes, and it made me think about our Christmas party. I wondered if we were going to all give each other presents."

"That would be a lot of presents to buy if we had to get one for every Brownie," said Jamila thoughtfully.

"Exactly," said Charlie. "So what if we all put our name on a piece of paper and put the pieces of paper into a hat? Then we each pull a name out of the hat and that's the person we make a present for." Charlie grinned.

"Brilliant!" her four friends exclaimed.

Just then, the school bell rang.

"Hooray!" said Jamila. "It's freezing out here — let's go in!"

Chapter 4

At Brownies on Tuesday night, Charlie told Vicky and Sam about her idea in the Pow Wow.

"Oh yes!" said Vicky. "We do that at my office every year – it's called Secret Santa."

"You could each make a small present," added Sam. "And then if any of you are working on your Craft badge, you could include it as part of your badge work."

"Tell you what – why don't Charlie and I write down everyone's names on pieces of paper in a bit," suggested Daisy. "Then we'll put them in my woolly hat and everyone can pull out a name at home time?"

"Excellent idea," said Sam. "Now, has everyone had a think about the Christmas present boxes? Who'd like to make one?"

Every single Brownie put up her hand.

"Brilliant!" said Sam. "And who has brought back their pantomime permission form?"

Lots of hands popped up again, and forms were passed to the Leader.

"Did everyone take a copy of the letter last week about the Christmas market?" asked Vicky. "If you need another one, just ask me before you leave tonight. We also have a form to give you about the Christmas party!"

"For the newer girls who haven't been to a Brownie Christmas party before, it would be great if you could bring some Christmas food along to share," said Vicky.

"That reminds me!" said Jamila, putting up her hand. "I've brought some biscuits with

me for my Cook badge work. If you like
them, I could make some more for the party!"

"Oh, yummy," said Sam. "Thank you! We'll
have those after we've done our next activity.
But first, does anyone have any news?"

Tayla-Ann put up her hand. "I've got a
new hearing aid!" She grinned.

"I didn't know you had a hearing aid,"
said Sukia, surprised.

"Well, I only got it yesterday," Tayla-Ann
explained. "I don't always hear what people
are saying if I don't look at them when they
speak. So my dad took me to the doctor and
she decided I should get one."

"You can tell what people are saying by
looking at their lips?" asked Amber, amazed.

Tayla-Ann nodded.

"May we see your hearing aid?" asked Sam.

"Sure!" She pulled the hair away from her

right ear and showed them a pretty red loop around her ear.

"Hey, it's even a Christmassy colour!" said Lucy.

"Do you like it?" asked Megan.

"I didn't like it at first," said Tayla-Ann. "When they first switched it on it was like everyone was shouting at me! I wanted to turn it off. But now I'm getting used to it and can hear people better."

"I think it looks cool," said Charlie.

Vicky grinned. "Right, girls. Time to learn a new craft!"

"Yes," added Sam. "Tonight we're going to decorate a little mirror with some glass paints. Come on – we'll show you how to do it!"

The Brownies got busy painting their mirrors. Some girls painted flowery borders; others chose Christmassy things like holly wreaths and bells.

"I'm going to give this to my mum," Katie told the Foxes.

"Mine's for my cousin," her Sixer, Emma, replied.

On the Squirrels' table, Charlie was the first to finish her mirror.

"Shall we sort out the Secret Santa draw now?" Daisy suggested.

"OK!" Charlie replied, following the Young Leader across the hall.

Meanwhile, at the Hedgehog table, Vicky was helping the girls with their glass painting. As they worked, they chatted about the Craft badge.

"I'd like to do it," said Abebi.

"You should! I did, and I really enjoyed it," said Ellie, who was flicking through her copy of the *Brownie Badge Book*. "I was wondering about doing the Toymaker badge next."

"Great!" said Sam.

The two Brownies chatted with their Leader about what they would need to do to complete their badges. After a while, Vicky put up her right hand. Soon everyone in the hall copied Vicky and fell silent.

"Thank you, Brownies," said Vicky. "Your mirrors look gorgeous! If you all tidy away now, there's just enough time for us to do some singing."

The Brownies rushed to get ready and were soon sitting in a circle in the middle of the hall.

"Please, Vicky!" urged Charlie, waving her hand in the air. "Can we sing some Christmas songs?"

"Good idea," agreed Vicky. "We'll need a bit of practice before we sing at the market."

"Any suggestions?" asked Sam.

"'Rudolph the Red Nosed Reindeer'!"
suggested Molly.

"Or 'When Santa got Stuck up the
Chimney'!" added Grace.

All the Brownies had great ideas and sang
enthusiastically. But after the second round of
"The Twelve Days of Christmas", Vicky and
Sam announced it was time to go home.
The Brownies put on their coats and
collected their mirrors,
taking extra care as
they weren't quite
dry yet.

"Don't forget
to pick your
Secret Santa name
as you leave," said
Daisy, holding out
her hat.

"And I've got your letters about the party too!" added Sam.

"Who've you got for Secret Santa?" Ellie whispered to Jamila, as they walked out into the cold night to meet their parents.

"If she told you it wouldn't be a secret, would it?" giggled Charlie.

"True!" Katie laughed. "But I'm really pleased with who I got."

"Me too!" said her four friends at the same time, before bursting into laughter.

Chapter 5

"I've got my first rehearsal for the pantomime today," said Grace, as they ate lunch the next day. "Caitlin and I are going together after school."

"Good luck," said Jamila, giving her friend a hug. "Hey, have you seen they've put up the tree outside the town hall? Everything's getting so Christmassy, isn't it?"

"The shops are full of presents," said Ellie. "And I've been thinking about what I'm going to make for my Secret Santa gift."

"Just make sure you don't tell us who it's for!" Charlie warned, giggling.

"Yes. But…" Katie leaned forward and whispered. "Would it really matter if we knew and didn't tell anyone else?"

"Isn't that a bit naughty?" said Grace.

"Yes and no…" said Jamila. "I mean, have any of you got one of our names on your slip of paper? I haven't."

The others shook their heads.

"Well, if we promise to keep the names a secret, we could tell each other who we've got and then help with ideas for presents," suggested Charlie.

"Shall we make that promise?" asked Katie.

The other girls nodded.

"OK." Katie looked over her shoulder and then leaned even closer. "I've got Danuta! I thought she'd like something sporty."

"You could make a sports bag for her trainers," said Charlie.

Everyone thought that was a great idea.

Next, Jamila told them she'd picked out
Tayla-Ann. "I was thinking about decorating
a hair clip for her," she said.

"Brilliant!" said Ellie. "I've got Abebi.
I'm making her some badges with kittens
on because she was telling me how much
she loves her cat!"

"That's really cute," said Charlie.

"I haven't a clue what to make for Ruby."

"She likes art, like me," said Ellie. "Why don't you make her a pen pot."

"Great idea!" said Charlie.

"I've got Leah, and I'm going to make her a friendship bracelet. So, that's all of us sorted." Grace grinned. "Isn't it strange that we got all the newer Brownies!"

"Really strange," agreed Jamila. "Only we've got to keep it a secret, remember!"

"Why don't we get together one night to make the presents?" suggested Ellie.

"Yes, let's do that," said Grace. "Hey – how are you getting on with your scarves? Katie and me are knitting every night."

"Me too!" said Charlie. "My gran sent me some wool and I'm doing stripes."

"I reckon we'll need our own scarves on to play outside once we've finished our

lunch," said Jamila, looking out of the
window at the frosty playground.

Caitlin and Grace told the others all about
their rehearsal at break the next day.
Wrapped up warm in their coats, hats and
gloves, the girls were enjoying the beautiful
winter sunshine in the playground.

"Did you meet any of the stars last night?"
Charlie wanted to know.

"Yes!" said Grace. "Trina Bliss was there!"

"Is she nice?" Jamila asked. "She seems
really nice on the telly."

"Oh, she was lovely," Caitlin confirmed.
"And so was Jez Simons – he shook our
hands. We got all their autographs!"

"We met Chester Chuckles as well," said
Grace. "He was so funny!"

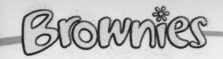

"Did you start to learn your dance steps?" asked Ellie.

"No, but we did meet our Dance Captain, Donnella," explained Grace. "She's great."

"What's a Dance Captain?" Charlie asked.

"She's in charge of the dancers," said Caitlin. "She makes sure that we know our steps and when to come on stage."

"Wow!" exclaimed Ellie. "That's so cool!"

"We watched Donnella and one of the other older dancers doing the steps. So although we haven't started learning them yet, we've got an idea of what we'll have to do. And the music is just brilliant – you'll love it, Jamila!" said Grace.

Of all the girls, Jamila was the most passionate about music.

"I can't wait to see the show!" said Jamila. "Ooh, that reminds me – Mum says we can

have our sleepover after the pantomime."

"More good news! Plus we're going to Katie and Grace's house for tea tonight to do some more knitting," Ellie said. "Has everyone remembered to bring their knitting with them?"

All the girls but Grace nodded.

"Hey, will you be there tonight, Grace? You don't have a rehearsal today, do you?"

Grace made a sad face. "Sorry, I do!" she said. "It's our first proper rehearsal this afternoon — my first chance to learn those steps."

So the best friends made the most of their time with Grace during break that day. The twins' mum came to pick the girls up after school, and they dropped Grace off at her dance practice on the way home.

When they arrived at the twins' house, Katie showed them her Sports badge project book as they munched on chocolate cake.

"I've found photos of all my favourite sports personalities," she explained. "And I have to show how I've improved at a sport, so I've been keeping a record of my netball training over the past term. I knew I needed to get better at shooting goals, so I've been working on my technique."

"How have you done that?" asked Jamila.

"Well, we've got a hoop in the garden now, and I practise as much as I can before it gets dark. Mum has taken some photos of me playing as well," said Katie. "And I've kept a tally of how many goals I've scored in matches this term."

"That's great!" said Charlie. "You'll be getting your Sports badge in no time."

"I wonder how Grace is getting on," said Jamila.

"I expect I'll hear all about it when she gets home." Katie giggled.

"Hey – is that your scarf?" said Ellie. She pointed to a multi-coloured stripy scarf folded on the sofa.

"Yes." Katie grinned. She held it up for the girls to see. "What do you think?"

"It looks great!" exclaimed Jamila. "And you've done loads. Mine's still short – look!"

"You'll soon catch up if we get knitting now," Katie assured her.

So the four best friends spent the rest of the afternoon happily knitting.

The weekend sped by, and at school on Monday, Grace and Caitlin were buzzing with excitement. They had so much to tell everyone about their rehearsal that, in the end, they just gave a performance of what they'd learned in the playground.

Everyone cheered as they finished their routine. Grace was still tapping out the steps when they met up for tea at Charlie's house after school to get their Christmas present boxes ready.

Once the girls had covered their boxes in festive wrapping paper, they added their assortment of gifts, topped off with the scarves they had all raced to finish over the weekend.

"How did you have time to finish your scarf, Grace?" Ellie asked. "I mean, didn't you spend all weekend rehearsing?"

"Actually, I only did a tiny bit of mine," Grace confessed. "Katie and Mum helped!"

"My mum helped with mine too," revealed Charlie.

"Well, I think they all look great, whoever helped us make them," said Jamila. "Come on – let's put in a little note to wish the children a Happy Christmas from the Brownies."

"My mum said the Christmas present boxes might be the only gifts these children will get all year," Ellie said, as she wrote her note.

Her friends nodded sadly, and thought about how lucky they were. They hoped that their presents would let whoever received them know that children were thinking of them from across the other side of the world.

Just then, Boo ran into the room.

"Hey, you'll never guess what I've just heard on the telly," she said. "It's going to snow!"

Chapter 6

"It has been so cold I thought it might snow this afternoon," said Charlie, as she joined her Six at Brownies the following evening.

"Me too!" said Bethany. "Oh, I hope we have a white Christmas!"

Once all the girls had arrived, Vicky collected their signed permission forms for the Christmas market and the party.

Then she made an announcement. "Before our Pow Wow, girls, would you like to put your Christmas present boxes on this table?"

The best friends rushed over excitedly, and added their boxes to the growing pile of presents.

Sam then called all the girls into the
Brownie Ring.

"Well done for bringing in your
Christmas present boxes tonight," said
Vicky, looking at the huge pile on the table.
"They look fantastically festive. We'll be
sending them to the central collection point
tomorrow."

"Do you know which countries they will
go to?" asked Abebi.

"We're not sure," said Vicky. "But there will be a newsletter sent after Christmas telling us all the countries where the presents end up. We'll let you know when we get that."

"Now," continued Sam. "Has anyone got any news to share?"

A sea of hands went up.

"Ashvini first," said Sam.

"Did you see on the news it's going to snow?" Ashvini asked.

"Oh, I was going to say that!" said all the other Brownies.

Everyone laughed.

"Yes, I did! And I was pleased to see you were all wrapped up warm when you arrived this evening," said Vicky. "Which neatly brings me on to what we are going to do tonight…"

The Brownies sat up eagerly.

"Tonight we're going to be making hats!" said Sam.

"What kind of hats?" asked Ellie.

"Ones like … this," said Vicky, putting a bright red pointy hat on her head, complete with a white pompom on the top and a fuzzy white ring of cotton wool fake fur around the bottom.

"We can wear them when we sing at the Christmas market," explained Sam.

The Brownies all cheered.

Everyone had a great time piecing together the red felt and fluffy cotton wool.

"Make sure the fabric glue is dry before you put the hats on your heads," Vicky warned, as the girls finished up. "You don't want them to get stuck!"

"I wish I was coming to the Christmas market on Saturday," Grace said sadly to Charlie, as they admired each other's hats.

"You're not coming?" exclaimed her friend.

"I can't," said Grace. "Caitlin and I will be at the theatre, rehearsing for the pantomime all day."

"That's a shame," replied Jamila, who had joined them.

Grace sighed. "I'm sure we'll have a great time, but I'll be sad to miss out on a Brownie adventure! Will you tell me all about the market when we go to the cinema on Sunday?"

The five friends had arranged to go and see a new Christmas film together. It was so exciting to have so many festive treats!

"Course we will," said Jamila.

Just then, Sam called out, "Clear your things away now, girls. It's time to practise our Christmas songs for Saturday!"

Once the Brownies had sung their hearts out, they had just enough time to play a skipping game. At the end of the evening, the girls raced out to meet their parents, hoping that the snow had started to fall. But, for that night anyway, there was no snow to be seen...

There was no snow on Wednesday either, but it was very cold. So cold that the teachers called the children at Badenbridge Primary in

from lunch a bit early to warm up with an extra singing rehearsal for the Christmas concert. And when school was over, Katie, Danuta and the rest of the netball team worked extra hard in their netball practice to keep warm. Grace and Caitlin had raced off for a ballet lesson after school. It was Jamila's afternoon to go to her music group, and she was glad to be cosy inside. Meanwhile, Ellie went to her after-school art club.

But the five friends were back together again on Thursday night, when they met up at Ellie's house to make their Secret Santa presents. They sat in the living room surrounded by pens, glitter glue, felt, card and paper, and sang Christmas songs as they got to work.

"I love your pen pot!" said Katie, as she admired Charlie's handiwork.

"Thanks!" Charlie grinned, sticking some smiley face stickers on to the pot. "I'm going to write Ruby's name on it in glitter!"

"Brilliant," said Katie. "I'm going to put Danuta's name on this too." She held up the sports shoe bag she'd made out of bright fabric. Katie had used some glow-in-the-dark shoelaces to make the drawstring at the top.

"Great idea," agreed Ellie. "Then she'll easily spot which one is hers when it's hanging up at school. Here – I've got some fabric paint pens you could use."

Meanwhile, Grace was weaving some sparkly silver thread into her friendship bracelet for Leah. Jamila was using the same thread on the hair clip she was decorating for Tayla-Ann. She held it up to the light and it twinkled.

"Hey, what do you lot think of these?" asked Ellie. Ellie had found photos of cute kittens and had cut them out to stick on badges for Abebi.

"Those are so sweet!" cried Charlie.

"Thanks," said Ellie.

"Hey, Ellie, have you done anything for your Toymaker badge yet?" asked Grace.

"I was working on it last night, actually," Ellie replied. "Do you want to see what I've done?"

Ellie dived into her workbasket and brought out a doll she'd dressed up as a Brownie.

"Wow!" said Jamila. "She's got a sash and everything!"

The girls admired how much hard work Ellie had put in.

"I've started making finger puppets too!" Ellie smiled. "I've done a Father Christmas one and some elves."

"You're so clever," sighed Charlie. "I wish I was as good at arty stuff as you."

"Everyone's good at something," said Jamila kindly. "I love cooking, Katie's ace at sport. Grace is a fantastic dancer, Ellie is great at art and you, Charlie, are brilliant with animals!"

"That's true," agreed Katie. "And talking of your cooking, Jamila, I'm getting hungry!"

"Good job I brought some fairy cakes for tea then!" Jamila giggled.

"Yes!" Her friends cheered.

"Come on," said Ellie, getting up. "Let's go to the kitchen and get some milk to have with them."

Chapter 7

The next day was very sunny, which meant it was a little warmer outside. The best friends began to wonder if the weatherman had made a mistake, and if it was *ever* going to snow! Even so, they were looking forward to the weekend – Grace because she had another dance rehearsal, and the other girls because of their trip to the Christmas market.

Saturday dawned bright and chilly. Vicky and Sam had arranged for all the Brownies to meet outside the town hall at eleven o'clock that morning.

"Don't you look great in your festive hats!" said Vicky.

"Have you all got your best singing voices ready?" asked Sam.

"Yes!" the excited Brownies replied.

"Good," said Sam. "Daisy will hand out the song sheets, then we can get singing! And hopefully we'll raise lots of money for charity."

"And when we've sung a few songs, we'll pop inside the town hall to have a look at the market and warm up a bit," Vicky went on. "Then we've been asked to sing some songs at Santa's Grotto!"

"Come on," said Sam. "Let's get going before we get cold."

The Brownies grouped together. Sukia and Boo were chosen to hold the collection buckets, while Daisy was in charge of the background music on her MP3 player.

"Everybody ready?" asked Vicky, making sure her own red Christmas hat was firmly on her head. "Let's start with 'Rudolph the Red Nosed Reindeer' – one, two, three…"

The Brownies had a fantastic time. After "Rudolph", they moved on to "The Twelve Days of Christmas" and then "We Wish you a Merry Christmas", followed by "Jingle Bells" and "When Santa got Stuck up the Chimney".

After their first song, people began to stop
and listen. Each time they finished a song,
the crowd clapped. Sometimes they joined in
with the singing as well. The Brownies were
pleased to see that lots of people put money
in Boo's and Sukia's buckets too.

"That was great!" Sam congratulated them
after their last song. "Now, I think we should
go inside and warm up – does that sound like
a good idea?"

"Yes, please!" the Brownies replied. They were all beginning to feel a little chilly, and besides, they were eager to see the Christmas market.

"Come on then!" said Daisy. "Follow me!"

The Brownies' eyes lit up as they entered the town hall. It was so festive! Fairy lights twinkled from the walls and ceilings, and there was a huge Christmas tree at one end of the room.

"Check out all those brilliant stalls!" said Ellie, looking around the room.

The hall was filled with tables covered in exciting things. Some had jewellery, others had toys – there was even one selling pretty boxes.

"There's a lady selling Christmas cakes and biscuits!" pointed out Jamila. "She's got candy canes too!"

"Oooh!" the Brownies replied, licking their lips.

"Just look at all those Christmas fairies on that stall," said Ruby. "Aren't they cute!"

"And there's Santa's Grotto!" exclaimed Danuta. "He must be inside!"

"There's a room for us to leave our coats over there," explained Vicky. "Once we've done that, we can explore the market. Come on!"

A little while later, the Brownies split into three groups – led by either Daisy, Vicky, or Sam – and toured the market. They'd each brought some spending money and found it easy to buy presents for their mums and dads because there was so much to choose from.

"That Christmas fairy stall has given me some ideas for my Toymaker badge," said Ellie, smiling.

"I'll bet!" Jamila grinned. "I wish Grace could have been here to see them too."

"Come on, everyone," called Vicky, beckoning the Brownies over to Santa's Grotto, where there was a queue of children waiting. "It's time for our second round of Christmas singing! Let's start with 'Santa Claus is Coming to Town'."

After repeating the songs they'd sung earlier that morning, the Brownies finished off with 'Frosty the Snowman' and 'Walking in a Winter Wonderland'. The children in the queue to see Santa sang along happily. By the time the Brownies had sung their last song, the queue outside the grotto had disappeared, and it was almost time to go home.

"Ho ho ho! That was wonderful, girls," cried a hearty voice. It was Santa, emerging from his grotto!

The Brownies gasped – Father Christmas was *actually* talking to them!

He smiled at their surprised faces. "Well done! Your singing really made everyone feel festive and cheerful. Have a great Christmas – it's going to be a busy time for me, but I know you'll all have a wonderful day!"

With that, he waved goodbye and disappeared back inside his grotto.

"Is he really Father Christmas?" Ellie asked.

"I don't know," said Jamila. "But he did have a long, white beard…"

"And rosy cheeks," added Ruby. "And a big tummy…"

The Brownies giggled. All around them, the market stallholders were packing away their things.

"Come on – let's help clear up," said Sam.

The busy Brownies stacked chairs, folded up tables and collected rubbish. The grown-ups were really grateful for their help.

"Do you know how much money we've raised?" Izzy asked the Leaders as they worked.

"Not yet," Vicky replied. "But we'll add it all up in time for Tuesday's meeting."

Sam looked at her watch. "It's time for

you to meet your parents outside, so let's grab our coats, girls!"

Once they had wrapped up warm, Jamila, Ellie, Katie and Charlie headed for the exit.

"You know I said I had lots of new ideas for toys earlier?" Ellie said to her friends. "Well, I was thinking about Grace missing out on today. She's worked so hard on the pantomime, and I was wondering – what if we made her a special present to say well done. We could give it to her after the show on the night we go to see it."

"That's a brilliant suggestion!" said Jamila, and the others agreed. "What kind of present?"

"I was thinking maybe a teddy," explained Ellie. "We could dress it up as a dancer."

"A good luck teddy!" said Charlie.

"We could do it next week when Grace is at rehearsals," suggested Katie. "She'll love it!"

The four girls giggled and followed the other Brownies out on to the high street.

The five best friends were disappointed to see there was *still* no snow when they woke the next morning. They soon cheered up, though, when they met at the cinema to see the Christmas film. As a special treat, the twins' dad offered to buy them all some snacks to munch on. Charlie went for popcorn while Jamila and Grace chose pick 'n' mix. Katie and Ellie decided on chocolate ice cream.

The girls chattered excitedly in their seats, waiting for the movie to start.

"How was your rehearsal, Grace?" asked Charlie.

"Brilliant!" said Grace. "We know all the dances and songs now. And Chester Chuckles's jokes too!"

"I can't wait to see the show," said Jamila.

"Nor me," said Ellie.

Just then, the lights in the cinema dimmed.

"The film's starting," whispered Grace. "Promise you'll tell me all about the Christmas market afterwards."

Chapter 8

On Monday morning, all the children in
Badenbridge let out excited cries when they
pulled back their bedroom curtains. The
town was deep in snow!

Katie and Grace pulled on their wellies
and crunched all the way to school with
their mum. When they finally arrived,
they found Charlie immersed in a snowball
fight with some of their classmates. The
playground was filled with shrieks and
giggles. Both girls immediately gathered
handfuls of snow and leaped into the game.
As more children arrived, they all joined in.
Even the teachers had a go!

"Do you think it will still be snowy at breaktime?" Grace wondered, catching her breath as everyone lined up when the bell went.

"I hope so!" smiled Katie, brushing snow off her sleeve.

At lunchtime, there was still snow on the ground, and everyone had the chance for a rematch!

After school, Grace and Caitlin whizzed straight off to the theatre for another rehearsal. This was fortunate, because Jamila, Ellie, Katie and Charlie went round to Jamila's in secret: they were going to make the surprise dancing teddy!

"Mum found this in a charity shop," explained Ellie, pulling the sweetest-looking bear out of her bag.

"She's gorgeous," sighed Jamila.

"How are we going to dress her?" asked Katie.

"I've brought lots of fabric scraps with me," said Ellie, putting them on the table alongside the bear.

"Brilliant!" exclaimed Charlie.

"We can make a tutu with this," suggested Jamila, picking up some purple netting.

"And a tiara with this," added Katie, stroking some silver fabric.

"And some shoes with that," said Charlie, pointing at some pink satin.

Ellie grinned. "Let's get started."

Jamila and Katie made the tutu, and then chose some stretchy purple fabric for the bodice. Meanwhile, Ellie and Charlie got started on the tiara, adding stick-on gems to make it extra sparkly. But the shoes were the trickiest bit – they had to use a lot of

fabric glue to hold them together.

When all the clothes and accessories were finished, the girls carefully dressed the teddy.

"She looks so cute!" said Jamila, as they admired their handiwork.

"Grace will love her," agreed Katie.

"Let's put her in this bag to keep her safe," suggested Ellie, producing a pretty red gift bag.

Charlie carefully placed the teddy inside.

"Come on – let's go and get some milk and biscuits," said Jamila. "I think we deserve them after all that hard work!"

As the friends sat down in the kitchen to enjoy their snack, they chatted about the trip to the pantomime.

"I'm looking forward to seeing all the other Brownies there," said Katie. "And then there's your sleepover afterwards, Jamila!"

"And the Brownie party soon after that," Jamila replied.

"And the Christmas concert at school," pointed out Ellie.

"Then it'll be the school holidays," added Charlie.

"And Christmas Day!" all the girls said at once.

"Lots of fun things!" said Charlie. "Hey, that reminds me – the news last night said it was going to snow some more. Mum said if the snow is too thick, the coach might not be able to get us to the theatre!"

"Oh no!" exclaimed the other girls.

Everyone loved snow. But not if it stopped them having adventures!

By the next morning, there was more snow in Badenbridge. The weatherman said it was the heaviest snowfall in fifty years.

"Do you think the coach will be cancelled?" asked Jamila, as the best friends arrived at the hall ready for Brownies that night. The other Brownies were playing Traffic Lights while they waited for everyone to arrive.

"Our dad said he thought they'd have the roads cleared by then," said Grace.

"Phew," sighed Ellie. "I'd hate to miss seeing you on stage, Grace."

"Come on," said Charlie. "Let's join in the game."

After a few minutes, Sam checked her watch. "I hope Tayla-Ann gets here soon," she said. "She's the last Brownie to arrive."

"Come on – into the Brownie Ring. We'll catch up on our news while we wait for her," suggested Vicky.

The girls settled down.

"Izzy – you first," said Vicky.

"I took this photo of a robin in the snow in our garden," said Izzy, holding it up for everyone to see.

"That's so cute," sighed Abebi.

"Thanks, Izzy!" said Sam. "Now – Grace and Caitlin?"

The two girls told the rest of their unit about the rehearsal they'd had on Saturday and how much fun they were having being part of the pantomime cast.

"We can't wait to see you both in the show, can we?" Sam asked the Brownies, who nodded.

"Which reminds me that I've got a final letter about Saturday," said Vicky. "We'll give it to you at the end."

"Will the snow stop us from getting to the theatre, Sam?" asked Ashvini.

"I've spoken to the coach company," said Sam. "They think it should be fine."

"Yes!" the Brownies cheered.

"Now," said Vicky, smiling. "Did you all have a good time singing at the Christmas market on Saturday?"

The Brownies nodded.

"You sang so beautifully! Lots of people came up to tell us how much they enjoyed it," Vicky continued.

"Yes," said Sam. "We also had a big thank you from the organizers because you helped clear up at the end."

Jasmine put up her hand.

"Did we collect much money?" she asked.

Vicky grinned. "One hundred and twenty pounds! Well done, Brownies!"

The girls gave themselves a round of applause. When they had quietened down, they heard the hall door open. Tayla-Ann stood there, looking upset.

"Are you OK, Tayla-Ann?" asked Vicky.

The young Brownie shook her head.

"It's my puppy, Elvis," she sobbed. "I was getting out of the car when he slipped out and ran off. Mum's outside trying to find him now."

There was a gasp from the Brownies.

"Not to worry," said Sam. "We'll come and help – he can't have got far."

"Yes," agreed Vicky. "Put on your wellies and coats – let's find Elvis!"

The Brownies split into three groups, with Daisy, Vicky and Sam each leading one. The Leaders had quickly grabbed some torches from the Brownie cupboard and were now shining them across the playground, where Tayla-Ann's mum was already searching and calling for Elvis.

But Elvis wasn't there. Or near the bicycle racks. They couldn't find him near the shed, nor was he in the staff car park. The desperate Brownies looked behind the trees and under hedges, frantically calling for the puppy.

Vicky called everyone to the centre of the main playground.

"All stand still and listen," she suggested. "Let's see if we can hear him."

They did as she said.

"I heard something!" gasped Katie.

"Where?" pleaded Tayla-Ann.

The Brownies fell silent. There it was again — a little whimper!

"It's coming from over by the climbing frame," Katie said. She rushed through the snow, followed by the other Brownies.

And there was Elvis! He was sitting under the climbing frame, his lead tied up in knots around the bottom of it.

Tayla-Ann quickly set him free.

"Aaah!" sighed the Brownies, as the little puppy leaped into her arms and snuggled up.

"I thought we'd never find him," said Tayla-Ann, hugging him tightly.

"Is he OK?" asked Charlie anxiously.

Elvis licked Tayla-Ann's nose and barked enthusiastically.

The Brownies laughed.

"Looks like he's fine," said Tayla-Ann's mum, wrapping her coat round him. "Thanks for all your help, girls. I'd better get him home and out of your way."

"Bye, Elvis," the Brownies called, as they left.

"Well," said Vicky thoughtfully. "As we're all outside and wrapped up warm, shall we play in the snow for a little while?"

"Yes, please!" cheered the Brownies.

"We could build a snowman!" suggested Grace.

"How about a snow Brownie?" said Daisy.

The Brownies started to scoop up huge armfuls of snow. They built a tall snow Brownie and Vicky and Sam found an old sash and cap in the Brownie cupboard to put on her, as well as a selection of buttons to make eyes and a smile for their new Brownie friend.

"She looks just like one of us!" Jamila giggled, as Daisy took a photo with her mobile phone.

"Come on, everyone," said Sam. "Let's go inside and warm up before it's time to head home."

The Brownies trooped inside and settled themselves in the Brownie Ring.

"Now, don't forget that we've got the panto on Saturday and next week is our party!" Vicky reminded them.

"Daisy's got letters for your parents with all the final details for both events," said Sam.

"And remember the Brownie Christmas cards you made?" asked Vicky. "Well, it's time to send them to someone who meant something special to you during the Brownie Centenary, so have a think about that."

"OK, let's all join hands and sing 'Brownie Bells' to finish," said Sam.

The children of Badenbridge Primary were surprised to see the smiling snow Brownie when they arrived at school the next day.

Everyone thought she looked great, but she was beginning to melt by home time.

"Good luck tonight!" said Jamila, giving Grace a hug.

That night was Caitlin and Grace's first performance, but the others had arranged to meet up for tea at Charlie's after school.

"I wish you were all coming tonight!" said Grace a little sadly.

"Me too! You'll be brilliant," said Charlie.

"Course you will," agreed Ellie.

"Thanks." Grace smiled.

"At least Mum, Dad and I will be there tonight," said Katie. "They told us this morning – it was a surprise. But it means I won't be able to come round to tea at yours, I'm afraid, Charlie."

"Never mind," said Charlie. "Just have a great time and clap extra loudly for us!"

"Come on then, Katie," said Grace. "We'd better hurry up or we'll be late!"

Jamila, Ellie and Charlie waved goodbye to the twins.

Jamila grinned. "Grace is going to love her teddy when we give it to her."

"I know," agreed Charlie.

"Hey, do you think that we should give something to Caitlin as well?" Ellie wondered.

"Hmmm," said Jamila. "You're right."

"Why don't we make her a friendship bracelet at tea?" Charlie suggested.

"Great idea," said Jamila as she, Ellie and Charlie skipped happily out of school behind Charlie and Boo's mum.

Next morning, Caitlin and Grace told everyone in their class about their first night

as pantomime performers. They described
what it was like backstage, how Chester
Chuckles pretended to forget the words to
one of the songs and how much the audience
had laughed.

"We even did a bow at the end," said
Caitlin.

"And Trina told us we were good," added
Grace.

"They were – really good," Katie pointed
out proudly.

Later, at lunchtime, the five best friends
talked about their Brownie Christmas cards as
they ate.

"I'm giving mine to Caz –
you remember the dance
teacher who gave us the idea
for Dance Dash?" said Grace.

"Good idea," agreed Jamila.

"I'm posting mine to Suzy at the radio station, because of that programme she did about the Brownies."

"She'll love that," said Katie. "Mine's for Sienna. I hope it gets to Australia in time for Christmas."

Sienna was Katie and Grace's cousin, who had come over and joined the 1st Badenbridge Brownies whilst she was on holiday.

"I'm sending mine to Gemma at the Fourth Agnestown Brownies – you remember, we met her at camp!" Ellie said.

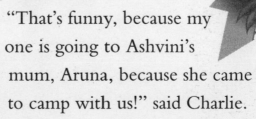

"That's funny, because my one is going to Ashvini's mum, Aruna, because she came to camp with us!" said Charlie.

"Hey, look," said Katie, pointing out of the window. "I bet they haven't got that in Australia!"

Her friends looked over and saw more flakes of snow fluttering from the sky!

By the end of the school day, the snow was falling so heavily they could hardly see their parents standing in the playground, waiting to take them home.

"Isn't it beautiful?" said Charlie.

"Yes," Ellie replied. "But if it carries on like this, will the coach be able to get through all the snow? And will we get to the pantomime?"

Chapter 9

On Friday, the weather forecast warned of more snow. But in Badenbridge, the sun came out, the snow on the roads turned to slush and then melted before Saturday morning. Which was just as well, because it meant that all the Brownies and Guides in the District who were coming to the pantomime managed to make it safely to the two coaches that were waiting for them at the Badenbridge Leisure Centre car park.

"All aboard!" announced the Brownie and Guide Leaders, as they checked the girls' names off on their lists.

"Right then," said Vicky. "Let's go!"

"Hooray!" The Brownies and Guides cheered as they left.

"I've got Grace's teddy," said Ellie, patting the red gift bag.

"And I've got Caitlin's friendship bracelet in my pocket." Charlie grinned.

All the way to Robertstown, the Brownies and Guides chattered with friends old and new, and sang Christmas songs to get them in the mood. The time flew by, and before they knew it, the girls had arrived at the theatre.

They had brilliant seats right at the front of the auditorium. The Brownies were each given a programme and they flicked through it eagerly, looking for Caitlin and Grace.

"I can't wait to see them on stage!" said Jamila.

"Shhh!" hissed Boo, who was sitting in the

row behind them. "The lights are going down. It's about to start!"

Chester Chuckles came on stage first. He was so funny that the girls' cheeks ached from laughing. Suddenly, he came down into the audience and said, "Well, if I'm not mistaken, I can see some Brownies and Guides in the front rows."

"Yaaay!" they cried back.

"What was that?" asked Chester, cupping his hand to his ear. "I can't hear you."

The girls cheered louder.

"That's better!" said Chester. "I think there's been a mistake, though – two of you are missing. I've seen two Brownies backstage. Do you know them by any chance?"

"Yes!" yelled the 1st Badenbridge Brownies.

"It's Grace and Caitlin!" shouted Charlie.

Jamila, Katie, Ellie and Charlie grinned at one another, thrilled that Chester had singled them out.

"Oh, so you *do* know them!" Chester laughed. "Well – if you spot them, give them a cheer! Meanwhile, on with the show!"

And then the pantomime *really* started. Trina Bliss looked so pretty, even in Cinderella's tattered rags. And Jez Simons was very cute as Buttons. All the girls had thought that Chester was going to be one of the Ugly Sisters, but they almost fell out of their seats laughing when they realized he was the Fairy Godmother. But they cheered the loudest in one of the opening scenes, because that was when, in a crowd of dancers, Grace and Caitlin appeared for the first time!

The Brownies waved to their friends on stage.

Grace and Caitlin beamed back but, like professionals, they continued to dance and sing with the others.

During the interval, the girls tucked into ice creams. "It's great so far, isn't it?" said Jamila.

"I just love booing the Ugly Sisters," said Katie.

"Aren't Grace and Caitlin brilliant?" said
Charlie, as she licked her ice-cream spoon.

"They're fantastic," agreed Ellie. "And I
love their costumes!"

The pantomime got even better in the
second half. The Brownies and Guides booed
the Ugly Sisters as they tried to stop
Cinderella marrying the Prince, who was
played by Stevie, a singer from a boy band.

Then they cheered as Buttons led the Prince, carrying the glass slipper, to Cinderella. They cheered even more when Grace and Caitlin joined in with the other dancers to celebrate the wedding at the end.

When the cast came back on stage to take a bow after the final song, the best friends clapped and cheered louder than anyone else in the theatre.

Once the final curtain had fallen, the girls grinned and turned to one another.

"What a great show," said Jamila.

"I didn't want it to end," Ellie replied.

"Hey, I've just had a thought – how are we going to get our presents to Grace and Caitlin?" wondered Charlie.

"Let's ask Vicky and Sam," suggested Katie.

The best friends explained to their Leaders about the presents.

"Tell you what," said Vicky. "Our coach is parked near to the stage door. Why don't we call in before we leave, and see if we can find Grace and Caitlin?"

"Yes!" the girls replied.

So, after gathering their coats, the Brownies did just that.

"I'll give them a call," smiled the lady at the stage door. "Just a minute."

The lady made an announcement into a microphone and the Brownies could hear it from speakers backstage.

"Grace and Caitlin to the stage door, please! Grace and Caitlin to the stage door, please!"

A few minutes later, Grace and Caitlin appeared, still dressed in their costumes from the wedding scene.

"That was fantastic," said Jamila, hugging Grace.

"You were both terrific," Katie agreed.

"And we brought these for you," said Ellie, as she and Charlie handed over their presents.

The two Brownies' faces lit up when they saw the special gifts their friends had made.

"Oh, thank you!" said Grace, hugging her teddy to her chest. "I'm going to keep her in our dressing room."

Katie tied the bracelet round Caitlin's wrist.

"This is gorgeous," said Caitlin, admiring it.

"Come on, girls," said Sam. "We'd better get back to the coach. Well done, you two – we're really proud of you. And we'll see you at Brownies next week."

"See you at our sleepover later!" Jamila said to Grace.

After saying their goodbyes, the Brownies and Guides clambered back on to their buses and set off back to Badenbridge.

Ellie, Katie and Charlie waited excitedly with Jamila at her house later that evening.

"It was amazing!" declared Ellie, when Grace finally arrived.

"Properly fantastic," agreed Charlie.

"Thanks," blushed Grace. "It was so brilliant to have you all in the audience."

"I'm starving," announced Jamila. "Come on – let's have our pizzas and we can talk about it as we eat."

After a delicious dinner, the girls went up to Jamila's room and got ready for bed.

"I really love being in the pantomime," sighed Grace, as she snuggled into her sleeping bag on Jamila's bedroom floor. "But I'm exhausted!"

Her friends asked her what it was like to spend so much time with celebrities.

"It's dead cool." Grace grinned. "I thought I'd be scared of them at first. But they are really friendly. And Donnella, our Dance

Captain, has given us lots of tips about our dancing. I'm really lucky."

"We're all lucky," said Charlie. "I mean — we all got to go and see it, didn't we?"

Just then, Grace let out a huge yawn. All the girls laughed.

"Come on," said Jamila's dad, popping his head around the door. "Time to go to sleep!"

"Goodnight!" the five best friends chorused, as he turned off the light.

Next morning, Jamila prepared a scrummy breakfast. She made cinnamon toast, boiled eggs, muffins and hot chocolate as the final part of her Cook badge.

"Yum," said Charlie, munching on some cinnamon toast. "Even this breakfast is Christmassy! Christmas is the best."

chapter 10

It snowed again on Sunday night and also on Monday while the girls were at school. Grace was performing in the pantomime again that night. So it was just Jamila, Katie, Ellie and Charlie who trudged through the snow from school, back to Jamila's to help bake cookies for the Brownie Christmas party the next night.

They measured the ingredients and took turns mixing the dough. Then Jamila rolled it flat and they all cut out the cookies and arranged them on baking trays. Jamila's mum slid the trays into the oven, and fifteen minutes later the cookies were ready.

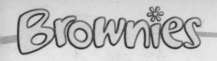

"They smell yummy," said Ellie, licking her lips as Jamila's mum put the cookies on a cooling rack.

"When they're cool, we can ice them. It will take a little while, so you'll just have to be patient!" Jamila's mum smiled.

The girls trooped upstairs to Jamila's room in the meantime.

"Hey, I sent off my Christmas card to Sienna this morning," said Katie. "And Grace has sent hers to Caz too."

"My dad's going to drop mine off at Radio Badenbridge for Suzy," said Jamila.

"I'm bringing mine to Brownies tomorrow," Charlie added. "To give to Aruna when she collects Ashvini from the Christmas party."

"Oh, that reminds me!" exclaimed Ellie. "I'd better get the address for the Agnestown Brownies from Vicky tomorrow so I can send mine to Gemma!"

The Brownies arrived at the hall on Tuesday night to find that Daisy, Vicky and Sam had decorated it with party streamers and balloons. There was even a small Christmas tree on the table where the Secret Santa presents were being left.

As part of the festive fun, everyone was wearing party clothes and the red hat they'd made for the Christmas market. When Caitlin and Grace arrived, everyone rushed over to tell them how much they'd enjoyed the pantomime. They blushed and thanked all their Brownie friends, pleased that tonight

they could be with them to share in the fun.

All the Brownies had brought party food with them. One table was laden with plates of crisps, fruit kebabs, sandwiches, mini pizzas and, of course, Jamila's iced cookies.

But before they ate, the Brownies played charades and then sang a couple of songs. After their party tea, Vicky and Sam announced it was time to open their Secret Santa presents, which Daisy handed out from under the tree.

The five best friends were thrilled to see how pleased Danuta, Tayla-Ann, Abebi, Leah and Ruby were with the presents they'd made for them. And they were just as pleased when they opened their own presents – even if they didn't know who they were from.

Katie had been given some laces for her sports shoes. They were hand-decorated with spots and swirls painted in neon colours. Ellie had been given a box of patterned jam jars to mix her paints in – perfect for an artist like her.

One of the Brownies had customized a comb with Grace's name on it, ideal for keeping in her ballet bag. Charlie has been given a notebook with a sweet picture of a guinea pig on it – one that looked just like her own guinea pig, Nibbles. Finally, Jamila's present was a gorgeous folder, decorated with notes, ideal for keeping her sheet music in.

All the Brownies were delighted. They had each been given presents that were perfect for them.

"Brownies!" called Sam, holding up her right hand.

All the girls fell silent.

"Time for our last Pow Wow before Christmas," announced Vicky.

The Brownies settled down, still wearing their Christmas hats.

"Well." Sam grinned. "It's been a great evening, hasn't it?"

The girls nodded enthusiastically.

"It's been a great year," said Pip, making the others laugh.

"We have had a busy one, haven't we?" said Vicky. "We've been camping, celebrated the Girlguiding UK Centenary, had our Dance Dash – what else?"

Katie shot up her hand. "We have lots of new members because of our open evening," she pointed out.

The newest Brownies in the Ring smiled at their friends.

"And we were on the radio," added Sukia.

"We climbed the clock tower at the town hall," said Holly.

"And there was the Christmas market too," said Izzy.

"Most of us worked for new badges as well," said Lauren.

"Good point," said Sam. "Which brings me to the final part of our evening."

"We've got some badges to hand out tonight!" Vicky smiled.

The Brownies sat up excitedly.

"First of all, our newer Brownies have completed their Craft badges – so could Abebi, Danuta, Leah, Pip, Tayla-Ann and Ruby please come up for those," said Sam. The Brownies applauded their friends.

"Next," said Vicky, "Katie has finished her Sports badge!"

Katie raced up and thanked Sam, who handed the badge to her. She couldn't wait to sew it on to her sash.

"You've all brought lots of delicious food with you tonight, but one Brownie has been baking for weeks to complete her Cook badge," explained Sam. "And that's Jamila – well done!"

Jamila smiled at her four best friends as she collected her badge.

"Finally, we have a Toymaker badge to award to Ellie," said Vicky. "It's one of the first Toymaker badges completed in a while – congratulations!"

The Brownies continued to clap until Ellie sat back down in the Ring.

"Well, girls," said Sam. "We've got lots of
exciting things planned for next year already.
But it's time to go home now … I can see
your parents are already waiting for you."

The Brownies groaned. They wanted to
stay and party!

"Come on." Vicky giggled. "Let's all stand
up and sing our last Christmas song."

The Brownies stood and linked hands.
Ellie, Charlie, Jamila, Katie and Grace smiled
happily at one another from across the
Brownie Ring.

Around the hall, all the jolly Brownies
burst into song:

We wish you a merry Christmas
We wish you a merry Christmas
We wish you a merry Christmas
And a happy New Year!

How Jamila got her Cook badge!

Brownie

1. Learned how to be safe and hygienic in the kitchen. Jamila's mum took photos of her working in the kitchen and she put these in a scrapbook to show her tester. Her tester also asked her questions about food hygiene.

2. Made breakfast for her best friends after a sleepover.

3. Made cookies and decorated them. She shared them with the other Badenbridge Brownies.

4. Jamila had to wash up and clear away after a meal.

Cook

How to make a Santa Hat!

You will need:

Red fur fabric or felt, cut in a triangle shape about 33cm long and 55 cm wide
Fabric glue
Cotton wool balls

1. Fold the triangle of red fabric in half with the right sides facing in.

2. Carefully put fabric glue down one of the open sides of the fabric from the top to the bottom. (Don't glue across the wide bit as this is where your head will go!) Make sure you put the glue on the right side of the fabric – that's the fluffy side if you are using fur fabric.

3. Leave the glue to dry completely before turning the hat the right side out.

4. Now place the hat on a flat surface. Put blobs of fabric glue on each cotton wool ball and then attach them all round the bottom edge of the hat. Then glue one cotton wool ball to the pointy top of the hat to make a pompom.

5. Wait until the glue is completely dry and then try your hat on!

> ★ **Brownie Tip:** Ask an adult to help you with the fabric glue. Wear a protective apron or old clothes and work on a table covered with newspaper.

Collect all the books in the series!

And look out for...

Brownies Book Bonanza

World Book Day is coming up, and the Brownies are bursting with ideas for how to celebrate it. From entering a writing competition at school to inviting a local children's author to visit them, the Brownies go book mad! Then the best friends have an idea – why don't they host a Brownie book swap? Books are the best!

Join the Brownies

Brownies do it all!

They do cool things to get badges like the Artist badge and the Computer badge, they have sleepovers, they make heaps of friends and have lots of fun.

Brownies are aged from seven to ten and are part of Girlguiding UK, the largest organisation for girls and young women in the UK, which has around half a million members and supporters.

To learn more about what Brownies get up to, visit www.girlguiding.org.uk/brownies or call 0800 169 5901 to find out how you can join in the fun.